Louie the Buoy

To Allain, Katie and Michael and the children of Sandy Hook Drive.

Design by Michael Ledet Art & Design,
 Hammond, LA.

Typography by Eugenie Seidenberg Delaney,
 No. Ferrisburgh, VT.

Digital production by Garrison Digital Color Inc.,
 New Orleans LA.

Production coordination by Kolleen Herndon,
 Metairie, LA

Print production management by Kaye Alexander,
 Westford, VT

Library of Congress control number: 2005928070

Second Printing
ISBN 0-9768320-0-3

Printed in China

Sandy Hook Press
210 Baronne St., Suite 711
New Orleans, LA. 70112-1747

Louie the Buoy

A HURRICANE STORY

by Allain C. Andry, III

ILLUSTRATIONS BY
Tazewell S. Morton, III

SANDY
HOOK
PRESS

2005

On the Mississippi Gulf Coast,
in the Bay of St. Louis,
stands a buoy named Louie.

Louie had been towed to the silver-green waters of the Bay of St. Louis on a barge by United States Coast Guard Lieutenant Manly and his crew.

They made deep holes in the sand to hold his four long legs so Louie would stand firmly in his position in the middle of the Bay.

He has four wooden legs painted with a special paint to keep away barnacles and seaweed. His platform supports a red wooden diamond marked with the number 14. On top of the red diamond a flashing light automatically turns on at sundown and turns off at sunrise.

On a nautical chart Lieutenant Manly marked the exact spot where Louie had been placed. He told Louie, "We will give copies of this chart to all boat captains using the waters of the Gulf of Mexico and the Bay of St. Louis.

"In the daytime when they spot you, and at night when they see your flashing light, the captains will know where to turn for a safe channel, either to the left for Jourdan River, or to the right for Wolf River.

"Remember, it is important that you never, never move, because if you do, the boat captains will be unable to find their way."

Lieutenant Manly told Louie about the big red buoy off Pass Christian that moved one morning, just to look at some mullet. Before he returned to his spot, three shrimp trawlers and a skiff had run into the sandbar,

and a big white schooner had
almost sailed onto the beach.

While Lieutenant Manly was talking,
Louie pushed his legs deeper into the sand.
He knew he would never move. The boat
captains could count on him.

Louie enjoyed being the buoy for the Bay of St. Louis. Schools of bronze colored croakers and silver mullet swam around him and hid behind his legs when redfish or speckled trout swam by. Flat brown flounders lay on the sand beneath him. His favorite fish were the striped

sheepshead that ate any oysters or barnacles sticking to his legs.

Blue claw crabs crawled sideways across the sand below him. Sometimes they would back out of their tight old shells, then burrow safely near one of his legs until their soft shells and claws had grown hard and strong again.

Seagulls, terns, and pelicans rested on Louie's platform. He liked their squawky talk and watched them dive into the water for fish dinners. The pelicans were his special friends, and he was happy there were once again so many of them around the Bay.

Fiddler crabs tickled Louie as they scooted and scurried around his legs and crossbeams. But remembering Lieutenant Manly's instructions, he was always careful not to laugh so hard that he moved away from his position.

It was lonesome in the Bay during winter. The crabs buried in the muddy bayous. The fish swam to the deeper, warmer Gulf, and the sea birds migrated to their offshore island rookeries. The days were short and the nights were long. The cold North wind was so strong it blew most of the water out of the Bay, leaving the piers standing over long, wet sandbars.

Even in winter, though, many boats passed by to keep Louie company. The captain of the shrimp trawler, the "Katie A", was a special friend. Whenever he passed by he tooted his horn, tipped his hat, and said, "Thanks, Louie, for showing me the way home."

Now it was summer again and Louie was very happy. But this August day was different. Louie wondered why more boats than usual were coming through the open bridge into the Bay.

Then his friend in the "Katie A" passed by, tooted his horn, tipped his hat, thanked Louie, and warned him, "Be careful, Louie, a dangerous

hurricane named Camille is heading this way and will reach the Bay by nightfall."

Louie knew that hurricanes were filled with strong winds and giant waves. He was a little bit afraid, but still confident this hurricane could not move him. The U. S. Coast Guard and the boat captains were all counting on him.

By early afternoon Louie was aware of a strange stillness in the Bay. The boats, birds, and fish had disappeared. The water began to rise around him. The wind grew stronger, and by three o'clock the sky was so dark Louie's light came on.

Soon howling winds uprooted oak trees and twisted the tops off of pine trees. Enormous waves filled houses with water and washed some of them away. Piers were ripped out of the sand and crashed onto the shore.

In the black water swirling around Louie, trees, chairs, fences, refrigerators, toys, beds and automobiles tumbled and tossed about. Suddenly a huge wave enveloped Louie. His light flashed several times, then went out.

"Oh, no!" cried Louie, "My leg's coming loose!"
He had almost pushed it back into the sand
when a large piece of concrete from the bay
bridge bashed into him.

All four legs were jerked out of the sand, and he was rolled over and over in the deep, black, turbulent water.

Louie didn't know when the hurricane ended. He didn't hear the wind growing quiet or see the water slowly flowing back into the Gulf. When the storm was over and the sun came out, Louie was on his head in the Jourdan River marsh, his darkened light stuck deep in the mud.

Not only had he moved, he had been washed several miles away from his position in the Bay. He was ashamed. He had disappointed everyone who counted on him. He hoped no one would find him and he could hide forever in the marsh.

But one day, as Lieutenant Manly was steering the U.S. Coast Guard cutter up the Jourdan River looking for missing buoys, he spotted Louie's four legs sticking out of the marsh. As the crew lowered the dinghy and rowed toward him, Louie burrowed deeper in the mud, trying to hide.

When they finally pulled him out and stood him upright, Louie said tearfully, "I'm so sorry, Lieutenant. I was not able to keep my legs in the sand."

The Lieutenant saluted Louie and said, "You have nothing to be ashamed of, Louie. On the day of Hurricane Camille I was in the Gulf of Mexico in my Coast Guard cutter warning all the fishermen and shrimpers about the storm. My ship was filling with water, my compass was broken, and I couldn't see any stars or buoy lights. I was afraid the terrible storm would sink my ship and drown my brave crew."

"Just as I had given up hope, I saw a buoy light flashing in the distance. It was you, Louie, in the Bay of St. Louis. I steered toward you, and just as I passed by, a giant wave covered you with all its force, your light went out, and you tumbled under the water. But you had already shown me the way to the safe harbor up the Jourdan River. There is no reason for you to be ashamed. In fact, because you were the very last buoy to remain standing in this giant hurricane, Louie, you are a hero!"

The Coast Guard repaired Louie's broken ladder, painted him, gave him a new light, and towed him back to the Bay of St. Louis.

They marked his position on the nautical chart, and attached a new number. "Because of your bravery, Louie, you are the Number One buoy of the Gulf Coast!"

Louie was very proud. He shoved his legs firmly into the sand and started to say in a loud voice that he would NEVER! NEVER! move. But he stopped, thought a while, and then quietly said, "Lieutenant Manly, if another hurricane ever comes to the Bay, I will try my very best to be brave and to stand firm in my position."

Louie is a buoy in the Bay of St. Louis. When the Coast Guard placed him in the Bay, Lieutenant Manly marked his exact position on a nautical chart. It was important for Louie to stand firm in this spot, it marked the safe channel for all boat captains traveling through the Bay and up the rivers.

Louie had a happy life in the Bay. He enjoyed the many birds that perched on his crossbeams, and the fish and sea creatures that swam around his legs. He remained firmly in position and proudly guided the variety of boats that passed him every day.

Early one August morning a friendly boat captain warned Louie of the dangerous hurricane heading toward the Bay. Louie had been through many storms and had never moved, so he was confident he would stand firm now. The boat captains could count on him.

This is the story of the trials, tribulations, and ultimate triumph of a buoy on that fateful day when Hurricane Camille devastated the Mississippi Gulf Coast.

A beacon/channel marker in the Bay of St. Louis was lovingly nicknamed "Louie the Buoy" by the children growing up along Sandy Hook Drive. They watched for its blinking light at night, and sailed, fished, and swam around it during the day. Amid all the devastation left by Hurricane Camille, the children were most concerned about the fate of the missing Louie.

The author, Allain C. Andry, III, above right, is an attorney and Savings and Loan executive in New Orleans. He and his wife, Judy, live in the French Quarter and spend as many weekends as possible in Pass Christian, Mississippi, at their home on the Bay of St. Louis. Mr. Andry grew up on the Mississippi Gulf Coast where his family spent the summer months. His three children and nine grandchildren have continued this tradition. He is a humorous and gifted storyteller whose stories have enthralled family and friends for generations.

The artist, Tazewell S. Morton, III, above left, currently divides his time between Pass Christian, MS and Auburn, AL. A graduate of Auburn University with a BAA in visual design, he had a successful career as an art director in advertising for over 25 years. In 1970 he returned to Auburn's art department to teach graphic design. While there, he designed a school flag that fellow alumnus Ken Mattingly placed on the moon during the Apollo 16 flight, thus making Tazewell the only American artist with work on the moon. He was also commissioned to design a limited-edition print commemorating the election and inauguration of President Jimmy Carter. His offerings range from spiritual to whimsical to abstract, created in a variety of media that include clay work, pen and ink drawings, acrylic and water color paintings, decorative and wood hangings and even painted furniture and fun "yard art". His one-of-a-kind art is appreciated by connoisseurs throughout the country.

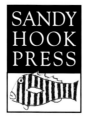

SANDY
HOOK
PRESS